The Great Fire

Weekly Reader Children's Book Club presents

The Great Fire

by Monica Dickens
Illustrated by Rocco Negri

Doubleday & Company, Inc.
Garden City, New York

The Great Fire

Chapter One

Peter was alone in the world. He was twelve years old, a strong, handsome boy with a quick smile and gay brown eyes. But his mouth was sad now, and his eyes were lost and hurt, for he was alone in London, alone in the world.

It was about three hundred years ago. It was New Year's Day, 1666. The church bells of the old City of London rang with the joy of hope in the New Year. But young Peter, sitting with his dog on the bank of the river Thames, close to London Bridge, was crying.

Bruno licked his hand, and Peter laid his unhappy head on the dog's curly black coat.

"Why did they die, Bruno? Why did they leave me? I wish they had let me stay at home with them. Then I would have died too."

During the last year, all London had been struck by a terrible sickness. It was called the Great Plague. If you caught it, you were almost sure to die. First Peter's father became ill. A cross was painted on the house door to keep people away, and his mother hung up a sign: "Lord Have Mercy upon Us."

But his father died one dreadful night when the wind lashed the little house like a savage whip and the rain wept.

A few days later, when Peter's mother felt the fever beginning to burn in her, she told her son, "Go away! Get out of the house!"

"I'll stay and look after you," he said. Already she was too weak to leave her bed.

But she shouted at him, "Get away from me —I don't want you here!"

He could not believe that his lovely, loving mother could say that. But now, months later, he understood that she had sent him away so that he would not catch the Plague from her. She had sent him away to save his life.

She died. He lived. Alone.

Peter's life was on the river Thames. The broad muddy waters were his world. His boat was his home. He had a blue and white rowboat called *The Fancy*, which used to belong to his father.

While the Plague still raged in London, it was dangerous to go into the City's narrow streets, where hundreds of people were dying every day. Peter and Bruno lived and slept in the rowboat, tied up against the sheltered side of London Bridge, huddled under an old blanket at night, the boy and the curly black dog, close together for warmth and comfort.

In the daytime, he earned pennies by rowing people across the river from the north bank where St. Paul's Cathedral stood high and proud over the wooden houses and shops, pointing its steeple toward God, to the south bank at Southwark, where farmers brought their sheep and cows and chickens to market.

Sometimes Peter rowed up the river to buy milk and eggs from the farms, and brought them back to the people who were living in ships anchored in the middle of the river to escape the Plague.

It was a difficult and a dangerous time. Someone had died in every family. No one knew who would be saved.

But now, on this cold bright New Year's Day of 1666, when the flags on the Tower of London snapped in the crisp wind, the sickness was gone at last from the City. Those, like Peter, who were lucky enough to be still alive must dry their tears for the dear ones they had lost, and get on with the business of living.

Chapter Two

"Hullo there, boy!" A shout from the river made Peter lift his head. Bruno jumped up and danced on the river bank, tail waving, barking as if he owned the whole of London.

A man and a young girl were coming down the river toward London Bridge in an elegant black boat with a sleek pointed bow and red cushions. The man was warmly wrapped in a fine cloak with a high collar. The girl, who was about Peter's age, wore a long white cape and hood made of white fur cuddling her pretty face like a kitten.

"Will you take her through, Peter?" the gentleman called across the water.

"Yes, my lord."

Peter knew Lord Hensham. He often came down the river from his apartments at Hampton Court Palace to visit the merchant ships at the docks beyond London Bridge.

The arches of the bridge were narrow, and there were many wooden piles driven into the mud of the river bed to protect the piers of the old bridge from the swift tides. This acted like a dam to check the flow of the river. When the tide was running strongly, the water level was much higher on one side than the other. It rushed under the narrow arches in a foaming torrent like a millrace. Shooting the bridge was almost like shooting the rapids. It needed a lot of skill to get a boat through.

Boats were always capsizing, and sometimes their passengers were drowned. Many people, like Lord Hensham, would rather let one of the watermen take their boat through the millrace while they walked safely around the end of the bridge to the other side.

Peter's father had been a waterman. In the happy days before the Plague took him away forever, he had taught the boy the difficult art of shooting the bridge. So now Peter carried on the same dangerous work. He called himself a waterman, although he was only twelve years old.

He held the bow of the black boat while Lord Hensham and his daughter Lucy stepped onto the riverbank, picking their way carefully through the mud in their polished boots.

"Are you sure you can handle our boat?" Lucy asked Peter. She pretended to be worried for him, but really she was laughing at him.

"Of course I can. I'm not a child."

"You're younger than me." She was rather a rude girl, but she always said rude things with a very pretty smile so that it was difficult to be rude back. Besides, she was the daughter of a lord, and lived in the palace of King Charles II.

"I'm not younger than you," Peter said, although he was not sure.

"I'm twelve," said Lucy proudly. "How old are you?"

"I'm thirteen." Peter pretended that he had to bend down to hold the bow of the boat. He could not tell a lie face to face.

"Girls are older for their age than boys anyway," Lucy said, and laughed, as if that settled it.

Peter wanted to say, "Girls talk too much." But she was a rich lord's daughter, and he was only a waterman's poor son.

"Come on, Lucy!" Her father called from the top of the bank. "Stop wasting time!" A lot of his life was spent waiting for Lucy, or her mother. "An extra sixpence for you, Peter, if you take her through double quick. I'm in a hurry."

"Why didn't you tell me?" Lucy said innocently. She ran up the bank and off to the bridge in her little red boots, to try to get to the other side before Peter.

Chapter Three

Peter jumped into the boat. Bruno jumped in after him and stood in the bow like a figurehead. No time to work the boat carefully and slowly up to the bridge. Peter's strong arms pulled the boat into the swift current in the middle of the river. He turned the sharp bow toward the bridge, drove forward, and shipped his oars just in time as the plunging water took hold of them and shot them under the bridge with shout of triumph and a lot of joyous barking from the boy and the dog. They never got over the thrill of shooting the millrace.

Lord Hensham and Lucy were already on the bank waiting for them. Peter hopped out and held the boat.

"Not bad!" Lucy called. "Not bad for a boy!" But her face was shining with admiration.

"Not bad? It was splendid!" Lord Hensham said. "The boy is the best waterman on the river."

He gave Peter two sixpenny pieces, enough to buy hot pies for himself every day for a week, and bones or fish heads for Bruno.

"Hurry up, Lucy. Get into the boat, dear."

The girl shook her head in the white fur hood. "I'm not coming with you, Papa. It's so boring when you talk business. I want to go to visit my dear Nurse Mobsby. I still love her, even though I am too old to have her for my nurse."

"You want to go to her house on the bridge?" her father asked. "You can't go alone, child." London Bridge was narrow and crowded with carts and carriages and people on horseback and people on foot between the shops and houses built top-heavily on either side. It was no place for a girl alone.

"Peter will go with me." She smiled at the boy and he grinned back. He was forgetting today's sadness when he had buried his face in Bruno's coat and cried for his lost parents.

Lucy was in a different world from him, but they liked each other. Although she teased him and liked to order him about, she was not a proud, demanding girl. She was rich and pretty and much loved. She was so used to people doing things for her that she took it for granted that they would.

"No, Lucy!" Her father tried to be stern. "You must come with me."

"No, Papa!" Spoiled, pretty Lucy stamped her foot in the fur-trimmed red boot. "I want to see Nurse Mobsby."

"What would your mother say?"

"Who cares? I'm in your charge today anyway, not hers. Are you afraid of Mama?" Lucy asked cheekily.

Peter stared from one to the other, his mouth hanging foolishly open, as it did when he was astonished. If he had ever talked to his father so saucily, he would have got a cuff on the head. Lucy only got a kiss from her silly fond father. He was a powerful man in business and in the government, and could even advise King Charles

himself, but he was as weak as a kitten against his beloved daughter.

"Come on, Peter!" Lucy grabbed his hand and they ran back to the bridge and plunged into the exciting crowd.

Chapter Four

The roadway between the tilting, timbered houses was so narrow that two carts could hardly pass. A farm wagon loaded with baskets of chickens had locked wheels with a grand yellow carriage. The farmer and the coachman were shouting at each other and waving whips. The farmer's wife, sitting among the baskets, was red in the face and clucking like her load of hysterical hens. The fine lady in the carriage, also red in the face under her white powder and feathered bonnet, had poked her head out of the window and was screaming at everybody.

The crowd that had stopped to watch the accident shouted back, laughing and cheering and enjoying the noise. There was always noise and excitement on London Bridge.

A baker, a butcher, a bucket shop, a tailor, a silversmith, a needlemaker, a saddler, a knife grinder, a bookbinder—everything could be found on London Bridge, a little world of its own, arching between the banks of the river.

Outside the tavern, a man had a big brown bear on a collar and chain. The man shouted and whistled and blew a horn to bring people around him. A crowd collected, standing back, although the bear looked sad and tame. The man's wife, who looked as miserable as the bear, began to play a thin scratchy tune on a fiddle.

The poor bear heaved himself onto his hind legs and tried to dance, front paws hanging down, back feet shuffling clumsily over the cobblestones. The crowd laughed and clapped and threw coins into the man's hat.

Lucy clapped, too, but Peter grabbed her arm. "How can you? It's cruel."

"It's sweet."

"It's horrible. When the bear got tired and wanted to drop back on all fours, I saw the man give him a kick."

"Oh!" Lucy put her hands to her mouth, and tears came into her eyes. "How awful! Do something, Peter."

The squeaky violin began again. The man shook the chain, and the poor bear struggled to stand

up. Peter waited, and when he saw the man kick the bear again, he rushed out and gave the man himself a painful kick in the shins.

The man yelled with pain and anger. "I'll kill that boy!" But by the time he had spun around, looking for him, Peter and Lucy had run off laughing among the people, knowing that no grownup can catch a nippy child in a crowd.

Panting and red in the face, they arrived at Nurse Mobsby's house.

Lucy's old nurse was now a dressmaker. She lived in a tall narrow house in the middle of the bridge. It was made of wood, with gabled windows in the high pointed roof, and it seemed to lean over the edge of the bridge as if it were trying to see itself in the muddy brown water which swirled below.

The children found the old woman sitting by the fire in a warm little room, sewing glittering beads into a yellow satin dress.

"It's for your dear mother to wear at the Court ball," she told Lucy. "Won't she be the loveliest of all the ladies?"

Now that the dark days of the cruel Plague were over, the Court of King Charles II and the fashionable people in high society had begun again their old pleasures of banquets and balls.

Lucy's mother, Lady Hensham, was a lady-in-waiting at the King's Court. She went to all the parties, with her beautiful black hair piled high and one ringlet hanging over her white scented shoulder.

Sometimes Lucy went, too, in a long brocade dress with a stiff swishing skirt and ribbons in her hair, and played at being a grown-up lady.

"But I'd rather be here with you, Mobsby dear." She sat snuggled on the floor by the fire, with her back against her old nurse's skirt. "It's so cozy here, and safe. I don't have to pretend to be a fine lady or a spoiled child, or anything except just Lucy."

Mobsby clucked her comfortable warm laugh, her quick needle flashing in and out of the gorgeous yellow silk.

"Your friends think so too."

Peter and Bruno were at the other side of the crackling wood fire, warming up for the first time since the cold weather had set in after their lonely Christmas.

"Do you really live in your boat, Peter?" the old nurse asked.

"Nowhere else to go." He did not look at her.

"After my—my mother died, I couldn't pay the rent of our house. Someone else moved in."

"Just think of it, Mobsby. No home. No mother and father." The light from the fire shone on the tears that came into Lucy's eyes.

"I wish—" she said. "I wish—Oh no, you couldn't, could you? No, you never could." She often asked questions and answered them herself.

"Don't make up my mind for me, child. Couldn't what?"

Lucy jumped up, lifted the frilled edge of the white cap which came down over the old nurse's ears, and whispered.

"Don't tickle." Mobsby shook her head and pulled down her cap again. "All right, he can come and live here, I suppose," she said in the rough way that hid her real kindness. "There's that little room at the back, over the river."

"Could he? Oh, it's a lovely idea! Oh, Mobsby, you are a darling." She threw her soft arms around her and hugged her.

"I couldn't pay," Peter muttered.

"You can chop wood for me, and run errands."

"Could I?" Peter's heart leaped. He put his arm around his dog's shoulders and grabbed a lump of his black coat. "But you wouldn't want Bruno."

"Oh—I don't care, as long as he behaves himself and doesn't bring in mud and dead mice," Mobsby said with a sniff, although she rather liked dogs and was thinking already of the mutton bone in her kitchen which Bruno should have this very night. The boy could have some of that good soup . . . And a new-baked loaf.

"Boys eat too much," she said sternly, to hide the fact that her old heart was glad at the thought of having a young person about her once more.

Chapter Five

So life grew better for the orphan boy and his curly black dog. Peter brought from the boat the few things that he possessed. A jerkin sewn for him by his mother. A knife that had belonged to his father. He moved into the tiny dark room that hung out over the river at the back of Nurse Mobsby's house.

At night, before he lay down on the sacking bed stuffed with the old dressmaker's odd pieces of cloth, he would kneel by the little window and watch the lanterns go out in the City, and hear a snatch of song as men came out of a tavern, and the hollow clip-clop of a horse taking a late traveler home.

The barges and rowboats lay at rest along the riverbanks. Below his window the black water rushed through the arches of the bridge, hurrying toward the sea.

He knew that the river sprang from a tiny underground stream somewhere miles away inland. He knew that it gathered water from other streams and rivers as it flowed through the green valleys to reach the end of its journey at last when it met the cold North Sea.

Each second that he watched, it was different water, changing, flowing onward, yet always the same to his eyes, familiar as a friend. He knew that his life would always be with the river.

Sometimes in the evening, with the lights of the City twinkling on the bank and the yellow flares on the parapet of the bridge making strange shifting patterns on the hurrying water, he felt that a great adventure was rushing toward him. The City . . . the river . . . Peter . . . Something tremendous was going to happen.

Meanwhile, nothing much happened except that his life grew happier.

"You're always singing," people would say, as he ferried them across the wide river. "I never knew a boy with enough breath to row so strongly and sing at the same time."

With good food and sleep, he was growing stronger. He could handle a boat like a man. His skill in shooting the bridge became well known.

"Where's Peter?" travelers would call across the water. "Peter! Peter! This is a new boat I've got. I don't want it knocked about. I want young Peter to take it through."

"Never saw such a boy to eat!" Mobsby grumbled. But she grumbled with a smile, and put more meat on his plate, and poured some of her beer into his mug "to make you grow."

She grumbled at him when he sat dreaming by the window when he was supposed to be chopping wood. She grumbled when Bruno came in from swimming, up the steps that led from the bridge to the river, and straight into the house to shake himself all over her scrubbed floor.

"You don't like us," Peter teased. "Shall we go?"

"Can't go today. It's raining," Mobsby would say. Or, "You have to go to Cheapside with the doctor's new breeches. Drat you, I need you."

Lucy Hensham often came to visit. She asked her mother if Mobsby could make her some new dresses, so that she could come to the house on the bridge to have them fitted.

When it was cold, Mobsby put some cider and

apples and cloves and cinnamon in a copper pot and heated them in the warm wood ashes. While Peter and Lucy drank the cider, feeling giggly and tingly, Mobsby told them strange shivery tales of goblins and witches and changeling children.

Their favorite story was the one about the Queen's son who was taken from his cradle by the bog fairies and turned into a frog. A bewitched bog fairy child had been left in the cradle in his place. Although he looked like the Queen's son, he grew up very odd. He was always shrinking to the size of a newt and swimming around and around in the wine goblets or turning into an eel, or appearing and disappearing suddenly with a smell of ditch water. The hair of half the servants in the palace had turned white with fright at his tricks.

The last straw was when he disappeared in the middle of his coronation, and the Archbishop was left holding the crown over thin air. His hair was white already, Mobsby said, so no harm done.

"And then what happened?"

"Wait and see." It was a long story that could go on forever. "It will see us through next winter," Mobsby said, "and the one after that and the one after that."

Life was so happy and safe that it seemed as if it, too, like the story, would go on like this forever.

When the summer came, Nurse Mobsby would sometimes pack a basket of cakes and sweets and her special little ham and egg pies, and Peter and Lucy would row upstream in *The Fancy,* and picnic in the meadows on the other side of the river.

They picked wild flowers for Mobsby, and laughed at Bruno, scrabbling madly at a rabbit hole while the rabbit sat safely underground and laughed at him too.

"Isn't it fun to have a friend to talk and laugh with?" Lucy said. "I like you better than those spoiled, dressed-up children I meet in the palace."

"It must be exciting," Peter said. "Seeing the King almost every day, and all those grand gentlemen and ladies I've never laid eyes on."

"Don't be silly," Lucy said. "It's boring. I hate dressing up and putting on party manners. It's a waste of time when you're young, and you could be lying on the grass like this with the blue sky to look at and a friend to talk to."

The summer was fun. The summer was safe. But still, underneath the laughter and the peace, Peter had the feeling of great adventure rushing toward him like the river's tide.

Chapter Six

It came in September. September, 1666.

The day before was Peter's thirteenth birthday. Mobsby roasted a duck, and Lucy rode down on her pony from Hampton Court Palace.

"I thought you said you were thirteen last year." She frowned at him.

"Well, I—you said you were older than me."

"But I'm not. I'm not thirteen till next month. So you see, there was no need to tell a lie, you stupid boy. Mobsby, he told a lie! What shall we do with him?"

"Roast his liver with onions? Put him in a basket and throw him off the bridge? Dip his head in a bucket three times and only bring it out twice?" Mobsby was always ready with fancy suggestions for terrible punishments.

"Come here and kneel in front of Queen Lucy, wicked knave Peter." Lucy's mouth was trembling with trying not to laugh. "We shall—we shall—stab him to death!"

From behind her back she brought a little flashing dagger and pointed it at the kneeling boy.

"Where did you get that?"

"Oh—I had it made," Lucy said carelessly. "By the King's armorer, if you want to know."

"It's beautiful." The dagger had a polished wooden handle, curved to fit a hand, and some carving on the bright blade.

"It's yours." Lucy suddenly dropped to the floor beside him. "It's your birthday present. Look." She showed Peter the blade. "It's got your name on it."

Peter could not get out the words, but his face was thanks enough. "It's the most beautiful thing I ever had," he said at last.

"Don't you go sticking it into my cushions, that's all I say," Mobsby grumbled, from habit. "Save it for the enemy, when you're a soldier."

"Haha! Have at thee, wicked fiend!" Peter stabbed at the fat duck, and mouth-watering steam and juices gushed from under the brown cracking skin.

They sang ballads and played games and danced together. Even old Nurse Mobsby, her cap crooked, her face red with food and fun, picked up her skirts and danced with Peter and Lucy. Afterwards, she fell into a chair, threw her apron over her face, and blew it in and out as she puffed and panted.

A knocking on the street door made Lucy pout.

"Drat!" She was not allowed to say that at home, but Mobsby said it, so she did too. "That must be William. I'll have to go home."

It was William, her father's groom. "Bad news, Miss Lucy," he said. "Your pony's lame. He stumbled over a stone and bruised his fetlock. You can't ride him tonight."

"Good," said Lucy cheerfully. "Then I'll stay here. Can I sleep here with you, Mobsby dear?"

"Your father and mother . . ." Mobsby began, and the groom looked worried.

"They'd say yes," Lucy said in the airy way with which she always decided everything for other people. "You ride home, William, and tell them where I am, and then you can come back tomorrow with another pony. Isn't that a good idea?"

She smiled and wheedled. She had discovered very early in life how to make people give her her own way—and enjoy giving it.

The groom went away. Mobsby brought out a jug of homemade cider to finish off the evening. Soon she took Lucy to her own soft bed, and Peter went up to his little room.

He slept, but woke before dawn and lay awake for a long time, too hot to sleep. It was a warm, sticky night. A wind was blowing across the river, but it was a hot dry wind that brought no fresh air.

After a while, he got up, pulled on his breeches over his nightshirt, and stuck his new dagger through his belt, for he loved it too much to go anywhere without it.

He crept down the stairs on bare feet, and called quietly to Bruno, who slept in the storeroom to keep an eye on the mice and rats.

Together they went out into the hot night. They walked between the sleeping houses to the end of the bridge and along the bank to where *The Fancy* was moored.

Peter loved to be out on the river at night. The water was like oil. The shuttered houses on the bridge were dark and mysterious, leaning against one another as if they were too tired to stand up by themselves. The City of London was spread out before him on the bank, its steeples and pointed roofs and gables black against the night sky.

In the middle of the river, Peter rested on his oars, his head raised, listening, looking, smelling. Something was wrong. Bruno's ears were up, and he was searching the night air too.

All at once, they saw it. Just a small glow at

first, among the houses of the City. Then they knew what the strange smell was in the air. It was the smell of burning. Sparks flew up in a sudden burst, and as the wind took them, a whole thatched roof leaped up in flames before their eyes.

And another and another. The wind was spreading the fire from house to house. A church steeple blazed. Flames rushed out of the bell tower.

The City of London was on fire!

Chapter Seven

For what seemed like hours, Peter could do nothing but sit in his boat on the water and watch the houses of London take light from each other, as if a torch were passed from hand to hand between them. A roaring, crackling sound was in his ears. The sky was glowing. Even the dark water was lit with a terrifying red glare as the houses began to catch fire nearer the waterfront.

He could see people running here and there like insects in a panic, black against the light of the burning houses. Some of them had run to the bank and were shouting to him, shouting to anyone who had a boat, untying the boats that were moored for the night, and pushing out into the water without oars.

Peter woke from his nightmare of shock, and rowed quickly to the bank.

"Take us across! Save us! Save us from the fire, in the name of God! A boat! Help me— save me! A boat! A boat!"

Terrified people were babbling and screaming. Some of them carried babies. Some had bundles on their backs, or carried bits of furniture.

One man was dragging a donkey. It kept trying to go back to its stable, but the man would not leave it behind. They stood in the middle of the road and tugged at each other.

Children were crying, dogs were barking, a horse locked in a stable neighed with fear, then kicked down the door and galloped away, swerving among the screaming people, its hoofs clattering on the cobbles. A pandemonium of noise filled the night, and under and above and through it all was the terrifying roar and crackle of the flames and the crash of falling beams.

A girl ran shrieking through the crowd with her hair on fire. Someone pushed her into the water to put out the flames. She rose up dripping but safe, and Peter pulled her into his boat.

A woman threw her bundle into Peter's boat and jumped in after it, clutching her baby. Another child jumped in after her, sobbing with terror.

"I'll take children first!" Peter shouted.

Four or five children were lifted into the rowboat, and Bruno growled and snapped at a man who tried to climb in, almost tipping the boat over.

It was a hard load to manage, top-heavy and dangerous. The frightened children made the boat rock as the current caught it in the middle of the river and spun it half around, and almost swept it toward the millrace under the bridge.

But Peter's strong arms rowed them through to calmer waters. He left them on the south bank and rowed to rescue more people.

As he rowed, he looked over his shoulder at the terrible, never-to-be-forgotten sight of the roaring flames and the sparks going up like rockets through the billowing gray smoke of the Great Fire of London.

Six times he made the difficult journey across the river. His arms were aching. Sweat was pouring down his face, and he could hardly get his breath.

Boats kept bumping into him. Swimmers in the water clutched at *The Fancy*'s sides and had to be dragged along. The river was now crowded with boats and rafts of all shapes and sizes—anything that could carry people to safety, away from the fire and the fierce heat that could even be felt from the water.

Each time he came back for another load, the air seemed hotter, the crackling louder, the flames closer. House after house blazed up along the narrow streets, until soon—

"Look, Bruno!" The houses at the edge of London Bridge itself had caught alight.

"Get away! Get back!" Peter yelled at the fat merchant, who was trying to get into his boat with an armful of moneybags.

"I'll give you a quarter of my money!" the fat man begged as he slithered on the bank, his face white as death in the light of the flames.

"Get back!" All Peter could think of now was the bridge.

"Half my money!" The fat man grabbed at the boat. Peter pushed him, and he fell into the water with his moneybags, kicking and spluttering.

The end of the bridge was blocked with fallen

beams which were blazing across the narrow roadway, setting light to the houses on the other side.

Peter rowed his boat close under the bridge. He could tie it there and climb up to rescue Lucy and Mobsby.

But the wooden steps that led to the water were crowded with people in panic. They were shrieking and sobbing. He could not climb up through them. If he rowed his boat too close, they would jump into it and it would overturn and throw everybody into the water.

Windows flew open above him. People threw bundles of clothes, chairs, food, pictures, wine bottles, even dogs and cats into the river.

Some of them threw themselves. They jumped wildly from balconies or the parapet of the bridge, and swam desperately toward the boats or the floating furniture, swimming for their lives.

Chapter Eight

All the houses at the City end of the bridge were on fire. Mobsby's house was in the middle, but it could not escape. Had Lucy and the old nurse got out?

As Peter watched, he saw the old woman in her nightcap and long white gown appear at the window. She was clutching Lucy.

Peter, holding the boat against the wooden piles at the bottom of the bridge, could see his friend's pale face, and her eyes big and dark with terror.

They did not scream. They stared down at him, as if they knew it was too late.

"Jump!" Peter yelled. "I'll save you."

He saw Mobsby crawl awkwardly out of the window and down onto the wooden parapet of the bridge. She crouched there for a moment, and then with a cracked shout, she jumped out and down, flying through the red hot night like a great white clumsy bird.

She hit the water with a noise like a cannon, and settled there like a duck with her nightgown spread around her on the water. She waved her arms and called to Lucy.

She called to Peter, but she was too far away from him and the current was taking her farther. Before he could get to her, a big barge came by, full of people. A man reached out with a boat hook and fished poor Mobsby into the barge like a dripping bag of laundry.

"Jump, Lucy, jump!"

Lucy had climbed down onto the parapet, but she was too frightened to jump into the water. While Peter watched, she began to crawl along the parapet, away from the house.

Only just in time. Sparks had landed on the roof, smoke curled up, and then almost at once the whole roof of Mobsby's dear little tilted

house was on fire. Flames licked out of the window where Peter had so often sat and dreamed. No more!

Trying to get away from the heat of the burning house, Lucy was climbing desperately on hands and knees. At the top of one of the piers of the middle arches of the bridge, where the water swept through in a torrent, a beam stuck out over the river. Lucy climbed along it, looking down in terror at the rushing water.

She slipped, screamed, grabbed wildly, and then she was hanging by her hands, with the fire above her and the river below.

Peter pushed his boat along the wooden piles, trying to get underneath Lucy without being swept under the bridge.

"I'm coming! Hold on!" As the boat reached the middle of the bridge, he felt the powerful water take hold of it.

Just at that moment, Lucy let go of the beam and fell, dropping like a knife into the water.

Peter stood up, felt his boat spin and plunge like a living creature, and then he and Bruno jumped into the water, as the boat shot sideways under the arch of the bridge and was smashed to pieces against the thick piers.

Fighting the pull of the water, the boy and the dog managed to reach Lucy.

She was almost drowning. She was gasping and choking, but her eyes were open and she knew Peter.

Bruno took her dress in his mouth, swimming madly, his front paws going like a windmill. Peter grabbed her around the waist, while with his other hand he tried to get a firm hold on the wooden piles of the bridge.

If he could not hold on, they would all three be swept to their destruction as *The Fancy* had been.

But the wood was wet and slimy. He could not hold on much longer. Letting go for an instant, he pulled his birthday dagger from his belt, plunged it deep into the wood, and held on. The handle fitted into his hand as if he had been born holding it.

In this way, grasping the knife, hanging on to Lucy and Bruno, he was able to keep them all above water until a boat came and took them way from the burning bridge, away from the burning city.

Afterwards he could not remember exactly what had happened.

Someone had lifted Lucy out of the water. Then two strong arms were under his. He remembered shouting, "My dagger! My dagger!" as his fingers were pulled free. Then he fell among people's feet in the bottom of the boat, Bruno on top of him like a wet seal.

That was the last that Peter knew.

Chapter Nine

When he came to himself, he was lying on the grass under the shade of a tree.

There were people all around him, camped in a meadow like gypsies. Children were running about. Cooking pots hung over small fires. Tents had been made with sticks and bits of sacking.

Everyone looked tired and ragged, but the sun was shining, and although Peter could not remember the past danger of that terrible night, there was the feeling that they were all, by a miracle, safe.

They were near the river, but upstream, away from the City.

The City? The burning City. Memory began
to come back. The City on fire.

A girl in a torn dress knelt over Peter. She
looked strange. Peter squinted against the sun
and saw that her eyebrows and the front of her
hair had been burned off.

"So you're awake at last."

"What's happened? Who are you?"

"Just a girl. Just someone like you who is
lucky to be alive. You pulled me into your boat.
You took care of me. Now I've been taking care
of you. You've been very ill. Worn out, they said,

with your work of that night, and your struggle in the water. My father found you on the bank like a dead fish, and brought you here."

"Why are we in this meadow?"

"We are all homeless. The fire burned for three days and three nights. They say it is smoldering still, and no one can walk on the hot ground. There is almost nothing left of London."

"Lucy?" Peter suddenly remembered, and sat up. "Where's Lucy? Lucy!"

At the sound of his voice, Bruno came bounding to him over the grass.

So his dog was safe, at least. "But—Lucy?"

The girl with the burned hair shook her head. "I don't know."

"There was an old woman too. My friend. My friend Mobsby."

"Hush," said the girl. "Hush now. You are still feverish. Lie quiet."

Peter fell back onto the grass and buried his face in his arms. Once more he was alone in the world! Just when he had found some friends, they were taken away from him.

Alone in the world again, he and Bruno, with no one to be his friend, no one to care. He was beyond tears. The sorrow was too great to bear.

For days, he lived like a lost soul among the refugees from the fire. They were kind to him. They fed him, kept him warm, and tried to talk to him. But he was silent and unhearing, as if he had been deaf and dumb.

One morning they tried to cheer him up by telling him that the King was coming.

Charles II, "The Merry Monarch," as he was called, loved his people, and wanted to help those brave and lucky ones who had managed to stay alive, first through the sickness of the

Plague, and then through the Great Fire of London.

"The King is coming," the girl kept telling Peter. "You must smile for King Charles. He doesn't like sad faces."

Peter knew that he would never smile again. The King would pass him by, proud and splendid, seeing only a deaf and dumb boy with a face too sad to look at.

Chapter Ten

The King came in a beautiful state barge, rowed down the river from Hampton Court by twelve oarsmen in blue and gold tunics.

The refugees in the meadow crowded along the bank to see him land. He walked among them with his high boots and his long glossy black hair, shaking hands, giving sympathy, picking up a child for a kiss, bending kindly to talk to one of the old or sick people lying under the sacking shelters.

Peter stood by himself away from the crowd. He would not look at his King. He would not look at the ladies of the Court who had come on the royal barge, carrying baskets of food and clothing to help the people who had lost everything in the fire.

Suddenly there was a girl's shout. "There he is! There's Peter!"

Across the grass, flying to him, her arms stretched out and her face alight with joy, came Lucy. His friend Lucy, whom he had thought he would never see again.

They hugged and laughed and shouted and asked questions and did not listen to the answers. Bruno danced around them, barking like a madman. Peter wanted to dance too. All of a sudden, he was alive again. The nightmare time was over.

"But Mobsby? What happened to dear Mobsby? I saw them take her into the boat, but I never saw her again."

"Don't worry. She's safe. She says she swallowed half the river Thames, but it doesn't seem to have hurt her. She lives near us now in a cottage by the water. A stone cottage. She's had enough of wooden houses, she says."

"So have I."

"Come on." Lucy began to drag him across the field. "My mother is here."

They found Lady Hensham handing out cakes to a crowd of hungry children.

"I've found him, Mama! I've found him! I've found him!"

When Lucy ran up shouting, and tugged at her cloak, her mother dropped the basket of cakes, and the children scrambled on the grass like puppies.

"It's Peter, Mama. Peter, who saved my life!"

It was like a dream.

Lucy's mother, smelling of roses, bent to him in her rose-colored silky dress and kissed him as if she were his mother too. Then he was introduced to the other ladies, and everyone said what a brave and remarkable boy he was, and that Bruno was a brave and remarkable dog.

And when the royal barge left, gliding away from the riverbank, as if the twelve oarsmen were one, Peter and Bruno went with it.

"Home with us. You're coming home with us, to the palace."

Standing in the bow of the barge to wave good-by to the people in the meadow, and especially to the kind girl with burned hair, Peter's hand was held tightly in Lucy's, as if she were afraid of losing him again.

"I lost the dagger you gave me," he said, looking down the river toward the blackened ruin of London Bridge, where the dagger must still be stuck fast in the wood at the bottom of the pier. "I am sorry."

"I'll get you another. I'll get you a sword. I'll get you anything you want. You can be my brother," Lucy said. "You can have the room with the four-poster bed, and you can have fine new clothes and roast boar and mulberry wine and raspberries and cream, and you can sit next to me at dinner, and dance with me in the Great Ballroom."

"I don't want to be dressed up and made to go to parties," Peter said. "I don't want to live in the palace, where everyone expects you to behave politely all day. I'd rather live with Mobsby in her stone cottage by the river."

"All right, you can then. I don't care, you stupid, ungrateful boy." Lucy stamped her foot and pretended to be angry at not getting her own way, but she was really smiling.

"I wish I could live there too," she whispered. "But Mobsby will be so happy to have you and Bruno again, although she will only say your feet are muddy. When we thought we'd lost you, she cried for you, but I expect she'll tell you that she said, 'Good riddance to bad rubbish.' Oh, lucky Peter. You can live with Mobsby in her little stone cottage, and you can have a boat on the river, and be our waterman."

"And take you for picnics?"

"With ham and egg pies."

"And rabbit holes for Bruno."

"In the winter," Lucy said, "Mobsby will make mulled cider with apples and cinnamon and cloves, and we'll sit by the fire again, just you and me, and Mobsby will go on with the story of the bog fairy prince."

"It was his coronation day, remember?"

"And he vanished and left the Archbishop standing in a puddle of water." They laughed. "And the Archbishop's boots leaked."

"May I share the joke?"

Turning, still laughing, they saw King Charles standing behind them. Lucy curtsied quickly. Peter had enough sense to bow.

"This is Peter." Lucy was not shy of the King. She smiled up at him, as she did at everyone. "He saved my life. He saved a lot of people on the night of the Great Fire, Your Majesty. He is very brave."

The handsome King smiled back at both of them.

"Well done, Peter, my boy. Brave like a true Londoner. Half the City was destroyed, but nothing can ever destroy the spirit of its people."